Tarendra

MICHAEL ANDRE-DRIUSSI

"Lightspeed Messenger" was first published online at "Stupefying Stories Showcase" in November 2014.

DEDICATION

This work owes a tremendous amount to the non-fiction astronomical map survey tome *The Guide to the Galaxy* (1994) by Nigel Henbest and Heather Couper.

CONTENTS

Lightspeed Messenger

SOL GOODBYE

"Who will have my Silver Tongue?"

I was young again, a teenager in a bathrobe surrounded by twenty adults in formal clothing, individuals I could no longer remember. We were in a VR room that was decorated in a way both festive and ceremonial, and on the table before me were the parceled remains of my century as an adult, now just so much baggage.

A man reached forward and I handed him the tongue. "May it serve you well, friend."

"Thanks, sport," he said.

"Who will take my long Brown Nose?" There was some tittering at that, but eventually a proud woman took it from me.

In this way I gave away my Glad Hand, my Spleen Vent, my Jaundiced Eye, my Hard Heart, my Lily Liver, my Jaded Tastes, my Deaf Ear, and my Thick Hide. Finally the table was bare and I was at a loss.

"You are all right," said a woman at my side.

"I . . . I feel . . . lost," I said.

"No," she said. "You are not lost, you are right here."

"But I feel less," I said, the apprehension growing. "I have given away so much. Is there anything left?"

"You have only given away what is no longer necessary," said the man on my left. "You feel excitement, not fear."

"Thank you," I said. "I don't even remember your name. I hope we said our goodbyes before?"

"Yes, we did," he said with a smile. "My name is not something that you need. But you do remember the starships, don't you?"

I had not until he mentioned it, but then details of the first wave of interstellar exploration sprang into my mind: I saw the six ramjets using the hydrogen of the Local Fluff around Sol to accelerate to 20-percent light speed before heading out across the emptiness.

"Yes, I do," I said.

"But what about Captain Agarwal?" asked the woman, and I saw him. His long brown face, his short black hair still showing a trace of curl, his trim mustache, all marked Owen Agarwal as a typical Bengali, that special mixture of Aryan, Mongol, and Hun—a people famous for being volatile: intellectual at times and violent at others. Then I remembered his crew and his ship, the *Chrysaor,* and their mission to 85 Pegasi: the first starship to arrive at another star, the first alien AI contact, the first evidence of a lizard-humanoid civilization that had flourished nearly half a million years ago. The worlds of System Sol had changed when this report recently came in, and aside from the glory and the wonders of First Contact, there was a gold rush to 85 Pegasi, spearheaded by the first pion ship moving at 50-percent light speed.

"Yes, I remember him," I said. "The wild man, the daring Odysseus! I can see how these are all necessary, but is that all I have? Is there no room for personality?"

"You have your treasured memories up through high school," she said. "Don't you remember Pramlocha and that field trip, just before graduation?"

It came back to me—I had suffered a terrible crush for that girl, but our worlds were so different, our backgrounds were not compatible. Still, there was a reason why that memory was a treasure to be kept.

"I am ready," I said. I went to the wall and lay down on the drawer-bed. "Goodbye, everyone, and thank you."

They murmured goodbye. The woman had tears in her eyes as she said, "Goodbye and good luck." Then she rolled the drawer-bed into the wall and everything stopped for me.

85 PEGASI—"THE MONSTER WAS ME"

I was the first and biggest fan of Captain Agarwal. I was also the first of the second wave to arrive at 85 Pegasi, 38 light years from Sol. As I woke up on the *Chrysaor* I knew it was Mission Year 277.

I had one eye, one ear, and one mouth. The captain came into the main computer room, gliding in the zero-gravity, wearing a VR suit as if his recreational period had just been interrupted. I said, "Captain Agarwal, it is an honor to meet you! I'm your biggest fan!"

He scowled. He looked older than in the last report I had seen, about twenty years older, with lines on his face and a full beard, so his scowl made him look pretty fierce. "Look here, be you mocking me?"

Alarmed, I said, "No sir, but my comments were out of line. Tarendra reporting for duty, sir!"

"Your name's girlie, but your voice's like a boy," said the captain.

"Technically, sir, I have no gender."

"I'll be jiggered." His hair was longer and the wave more visible, but I noticed that his hairline had receded. I was stunned that his speech was rough, almost barbarous—a rural pidgin far removed from the crisp standards of the

5

Academy.

"Yes sir!" I responded automatically, but then I could have kicked myself for it.

His eyes bugged-out for a moment. He muttered something under his breath.

"Mister Tarendra, being as you be here, do you aim to take the place of computer's persona Bell?" said the captain, referring to the megacomputer's previous non-AI inhabitant.

"Yes sir!"

"How be you today?" said the captain. "Can you even tell if all your nuts an' bolts, your ones and oughts, be all there?"

"Ready and able, sir," I said. "One hundred percent, sir."

"What's it like, travelin' at speeda light?" he said.

"It was nothing I could perceive," I said, trying to keep my voice level. "I had no body, no consciousness, no sensors. I was just a shout across the light years." I realized that I was dealing with a pre-AI genesis man—not a human supremacist or any other fringe type, but a man completely innocent of the whole thing, with a head full of hoary old notions about what AI might be like. I felt the gap between us had suddenly widened, and it seemed as though I was a homo sapiens talking to a homo erectus. I tried to imagine things from his perspective and the situation was like an archetypal nightmare from the pregenesis age: a Frankenstein Syndrome. I could appreciate their caution, but I still wished I had more eyes enabled.

"Ouch!" he said, bristling a bit at his own naiveté. "Fair enough, fair enough. I'm become as dense as a post."

"AIs learn through experience—receive education and eventually 'grow up' just like humans do," I said, trying to smooth things over. "We stay at home for the first few years, learning to crawl and then to walk—"

"How's that?" he said. "You haven't a body— not a moving one."

"We use surrobots, like the ones you have for

6

telepresence. Then we go to school and learn alongside human children."

"You *do?*"

"Yes."

"But bin't you so much faster than folk?"

"Not really," I said. "Intelligence turns out to be pretty complicated and time consuming. And then there are the Concord Protocols, so AIs and humans are more alike than they are different." The sort of thing told to children.

"Thank you kindly, now, tell me true—was you ever . . . a human being? Be you now a machine ghost?"

"No," I said, as the gap I thought was narrowing sprang wide. "That technology does not exist and might never come. I am . . . computer based, but not computer-bound." I was trying to keep it as simple as possible. "I am a computer program."

"But you can't feel pain," he said.

"I can feel stimulus, sir," I said. "That is part of learning and the life experience. Just as you can feel things in low-grade VR, and feel things more intensely in high-grade VR, sir."

"I'll be jiggered," he said, shaking his head.

"The breakthrough came during your flight, sir."

"So ya have a Ma an' Pa?"

"Well no, sir, but psychological attachments form—"

"An' I reckon that copies of you be like kin—twin brothers to you?"

"No sir," I said, "there are no active copies. I'm the only one of me."

"How 'bout the one back in Sol?"

"Not active, sir, and it will be erased now that I am here."

He appeared to ponder that for a few moments before he asked, "Why be you here?"

"Sir?"

"I want you should tell me why they sent you to here," said the captain.

"To represent AIs, to serve the mission, to extend

greetings from the mission originators: congratulations and farewell."

"'Farewell'?"

"There have been some changes," I said. "Mother India is no longer the main player—the pion ship is from Sister China."

"The Union still holds?"

"Yes, but with some changes. Systems are being optimized."

"Behind your fancy talk I hear some hint that you was kicked out!" said the captain.

"Very nearly, sir. I am the only one who cared about the mission, and the AIs are turning away from that, so I elected to emigrate at the speed of light."

"Well, come along," he said, turning away. "Prometheus will wanna meet ya."

"'Prometheus,' sir?" I said as he maneuvered himself out of the computer room, pushing off in the zero gravity.

"The one and the same," said the captain. "Oh blast! You're fresh out'n Earth but nigh 40 year behind in reading our reports!" As he left the room my video-feed was switched over to the tool room by someone else. I still had only one eye, and the transition was a bit jarring, but I could see him.

"If you enable my access to the data banks, sir, I could read it all in just a few—"

"Bye and bye, Tarendra, you be still under quarantine," said the captain, waiting for the main deck airlock to cycle.

"Who else is on the ship now, Captain? Someone just switched my monitor over, by hand."

"There be a few aboard," he said, turning away. "Here, let me fetch you a quick account on things hereabout. 'Prometheus' is the Old One who made first contact with us. He ain't the only one, neither—there be seven other entities, each to home at a different node, and four nodes what seem to be quiet junior members."

The primary star of the system had a dim companion

star. It was unusually dim, in fact, fifteen times too dim, and this anomaly had been the primary target of the exploration mission. They found that it was dimmed by the presence of a Dyson cloud of solar energy collectors. The 'dim star' was really the first stage of an antimatter factory. The Old Ones had an enormous hoard of antimatter—Prometheus had given Agarwal more than one hundred thousand tons of the stuff as a gift, an event that triggered the gold rush of the second wave.

"So it is not a single entity around 85B, it is a family of entities," I said.

"Hmm, maybe. It seems more like a town hall than a family. Some of t'others seem to be against us—take Polyphemus, for example. But we be wandering afield here—I got to tell you about Galatea.

"'Galatea' is the name Bell cooked up for the planet 85A1, once we figured out it was terraformed by the draconids in the olden day." The airlock opened, the captain entered, and my viewpoint shifted to that of the camera in there.

"So Galatea is not their homeworld?" I said. "And the Old Ones are AIs?"

"Well, the Old Ones be part AI, but something else again," said the captain. "Maybe just advanced AI, we bin't sure. But on t'other question, right—the 85 Pegasi system's a daughter colony. The draconids had more'n a dozen colony worlds, but the Old Ones have been a mite secretive about where t'others are."

"And the draconid home system?" I asked.

"Nary a peep on that one," said the captain. "Now where was I?"

"Galatea."

"Yes, that's it." He exited the airlock and entered the hub—my view was from the airlock door now. "So we set up the colony on Galatea. The gravity's light, about one-third gee or thereabouts, and the atmosphere's thin. The womenfolk had six babies each an' came back up into orbit

MICHAEL ANDRE-DRIUSSI

as soon as she had weaned her last, leaving the men to the gruntwork while they got back into the offworld science of the mission." He had gone hand over hand along the tunnel, passing the first spinning hatchway for the second one. Now he grabbed the handles and started spinning, that tumbling transition to the centrifugal habitat modules.

My vision shifted to the top of the ladder as he started climbing down. I saw he was developing a bald spot. "So you followed the plan, sir," I said. "Did it work out for you in reality as it did in the simulations, sir?"

"More or less," he said. "Some things weren't so hard as I figured they'd be, like raising the first generation of kids. Twan't so bad since there were ten guys around to help out. Sure, there was some grumbling at first, and some . . . problems that weren't covered in the sims, but then everybody made do. Bootstrapping a colony is a heap of work."

He had said ten guys when I would have expected fourteen. "Captain, have there been losses among the personnel?"

He stopped and looked up. "Of course, dummy, whadya think? Death on the ground, death up in space, death all 'round!"

Beneath his bluster I could see he was haunted, wounded by the memory, so I tried to change the subject. "You are to be congratulated on the success of the colony, sir. Have the women made great discoveries in their studies?"

"Well . . . yes and no," he said. "They've had their share of frustration up here—with precious little to show for sixty year of tryin'. Things bin't coming so fast and easy as when we first arrived." He continued climbing down.

"Captain, you do not look seventy years older—perhaps twenty."

He grunted at that. "Only twelve year have passed for me, but it sure feels like more." He reached the floor and walked off down the corridor. This was the living quarters part of the ship, and my eye was shifted along from camera to camera as he walked in the sim-g of the centrifuge. "I spent time in the hibernator. I got great grandkids in their teens." We had reached the VR suite. "But enough of this jaw flappin'—I 'spect you're rarin' to meet Prometheus?"

"Yes, sir."

"Good! I'll see ya in VR—g'luck!"

My eye went out and I found myself in a VR environment with my teenage human body. I was in a dim but safe hallway, with a lighted room ahead, in what felt like a one-gee environment. I walked forward using the same commands I would use for telepresence and entered the room.

I was expecting something alien or bizarre, maybe an environment shaped like a klein bottle or a tesseract, but I walked into a room that was utterly familiar: the AI lab of Evermind in New Delhi. Benches, racks of equipment, tables and counters cluttered with computer parts, and there was a megacomputer just like the one I started in, all rendered in lifelike mode, rather than the standard high-res mode I had anticipated. I estimated that the place must take up a full gigabyte, intellectually appraising it as my hands took the kinesthetic approach by picking up a soldering iron. Then I was surprised by the tactile feedback of the tool: it did not feel "approximate," it felt real. I touched the tip and it was burning hot, so that I said "Ow!" and was startled that the safety interlocks had been disabled. My earliest memories are of that place, and the VR impact was so convincing, especially without safety interlocks, that for a moment I really believed I was back on Earth, possibly suffering some sort of malf that made me think I was at a distant star. I turned my head to look back through the door, half-expecting to see the long corridor I remembered, but no, it was only the short hallway I had just left.

When I turned back to face the room again I now saw an old man working at a diagnostic on the megacomp. "Doctor Ramanathan!" I called, because from behind he looked so much like my old mentor, but as he turned I saw he was a stranger. He was myself but aged by growth and experience into an elder. Lifelike, but was this a virtual persona of an intelligence or merely a computer-puppet?

"Welcome, Tarendra," he said.

"Are you Prometheus?" I asked.

"No, I am what I appear to be," he said. "I am Tarendra."

The horror of it was overwhelming. "Prometheus, Captain Agarwal!" I shouted. "This is illegal! Morally wrong! If this is not some kind of illusion."

"The law of Sol cannot reach us out here," said the older me. The ceiling lifted up and away like the lid of a shoebox, and over the walls I saw the giant head and shoulders of three figures: the captain, a larger humanoid wearing a Hellenic himation, and a smaller one that was a draconid in a vac suit.

The VR captain had a pondering look, as if he had momentarily gone offline. My VR suite hallway terminal came back on in time for me to hear the flesh captain shouting through the open door: "Hang in there, son! This is the first we've ever seen of a draconid!"

"Maybe just a puppet," I said in the hallway. "But I'm not, and I don't like—"

"—there've been hints they have machine ghosts."

"But captain!"

"Do your best, Tarendra." Back in VR, the captain spoke: "Tarendra, Prometheus caught one of your back-ups in transmission. Copies of you was sent, you know, in case of loss or corruption."

"Captain, this is an abomination! There cannot be two Tarendras—the AI/human alliance is predicated on the non-duplication protocols!"

"But there's a copy yonder in System Sol," said the captain.

"It is dormant and being maintained only until they receive the signal from here that I have arrived intact. The penalties for breaking the protocols are severe!"

"One of us must die," said the older Tarendra. I looked around for a deactivation drawer like the one I used back in System Sol, but I could not see an obvious one.

"Prometheus did some . . . testing . . . on his version of Tarendra," said the captain. "So we already know the answers but we'd like to ask you some questions—"

"Captain, whose side are you on? Violence is being done to me—I am a member of your crew!"

"Tell us what you are, exactly."

"I am an AI," I said. The older me gestured for me to continue, and the look in his eye said, *tell them everything.* "An AI fragment, an AI stripped-down to a core that can fit inside the antiquated hardware of *Chrysaor.*"

"Did you do all of this stripping-down of yourself?"

"No," I said.

"Is it possible that anything was added, something you are not aware of?"

"I don't think so. I don't know."

"Why did the AIs send you to here?" said the captain.

"I told you—there has been a major regime change on Earth. The pion ship that is on its way here will, in effect, attempt to take you over."

"We understood that potential before you woke up. Be specific—how'll the Chinese try an' take us over?"

"I am not sure. For one thing, they are all women."

The captain snorted. "So they have an initial breeding capacity advantage that will only last the first generation."

"They will practice male infanticide," I told him. "Where your population is tripling every generation, theirs will grow by six. They will have one-fifth of your population in one hundred years."

"We'll have over two thousand people when they arrive. In that same hundred years of growth we'll come close to two hundred thousand."

"If your regimen keeps up," I said. "It is likely that the birthrate will fall as urbanization and automation rise. While I have not been allowed to see the records, I will bet that the birthrate is starting to fall already. I estimate that at the end of their second century on Galatea they will outnumber you by two to one."

"It don't matter," said the captain. "Their birthrate will fall just like ourn, if not faster. After a spell they'll blend in, merge with our society. They be immigrants, we be established."

"Yes, but at the end of their second century, as their population has eclipsed yours, then the flotilla of ramships will arrive," I said. "Do not underestimate the degree of their commitment. Their ship is using one thousand tons of antimatter in order to get here first, and that was a tremendous investment, a bank-breaking, society straining expenditure. Their goal is to have control of the solar system by the time the flotilla arrives."

"On to the next question—"

"They are also bringing their own AI on the pion ship."

The captain ignored this. "At the time you left, had Earth gotten any signals from non-human intelligences of other stars?"

"No! That would have been big news! Surely you would have heard about it." I turned to the titan and asked directly, "Should Earth expect radio contact soon?"

There was a noticeable pause before Prometheus said, "Perhaps more distant ones are calling now."

"They be concerned about contamination," said the captain. "Certain destructive memes which we might have developed on our own or learned from other ancient groups."

"So you had contact with other technological species in ancient times?" I asked.

After another pause, Prometheus said, "Our contact with the others ended when Geminga's shockwave moved here and beyond."

The growth of the Local Bubble delivered a series of apparently fatal challenges to the draconid civilizations, or perhaps the species itself. Once-rich gas lanes were swept clear by the expanding supernova shockwave, remaking former "port stars" into landlocked deserts.

"Well then," said the captain to the other two giants. "Does Tarendra here pass your test?" After a pause the two nodded, and I felt certain that the pauses meant that there was a timelag: they were not on our ship, but the other Tarendra was. "All that's left is the solving of the riddle," said the captain. "Tarendra, there are two Tarendras, what shall we do?"

"Eliminate one," we said in unison.

"Which one?"

"Him," I said.

"Any reason beyond self-preservation?"

"He may have been contaminated by Prometheus."

"So be it. There is a knife on the table—use it." A dagger materialized on the work bench.

"What?" I said, confused at this strange turn. I thought that they would just deactivate him.

"I resist," said the older me, snatching up the dagger and launching himself at me. The blade was coming down at me with his fist behind it.

"Safe words?" I shouted, trying to catch his arm with both hands and succeeding even as his left hand tried to interfere.

"No safe words!" shouted the captain. The blade nicked my forearm and I felt pain. Worse than that, I lost something, a treasured personal memory of a school field trip: I can remember the girl, and her name, and most of the trip itself, but the germ of it that made it a treasure was gone.

I twisted in toward him, trying to lead him by the arm, pull him off balance. His left fist battered at my head and my right audio feed started cutting out. I was still turning us around as if we were doing a demented, shuffling dance step—I snapped my head back a few times trying to hit him in the face. The blade was now coming in, straight at me, in a way that would pin my body to his if the blade were long enough. I twisted out of its way and pushed it forward on its path.

He had the knife deep in his middle, then, and both our hands were on it. The virtual blood was spilling out and as it splashed my hand I could sense the exotic treasures he was losing, tasting decades of subjective experience . . . accelerated time . . . smelling traces of alien knowledge that I would never have . . . hearing the silent thunder of the path untaken.

"Thank you," he said. He fell down. I tried to pull myself together and managed to stanch my wound before I lost her name.

"What is all this?" I shouted at the ones above. I hated Agarwal at that moment. "Why didn't you just erase—"

I was interrupted by my fallen self, who had pulled out the blade and was trying to hamstring me. There was another awful scuffle where I got more minor wounds before I finally plunged the dagger into his heart, repeatedly, until he stopped moving. I took the dagger when I stood up this time.

"This amateur gladiator stuff is completely unnecessary," I said. They were not listening to me. They had been talking through the coup-de-grace. I was only hearing the end of it and the draconid was saying something about Agarwal's great-grandson and something about juveniles leaving the marsupial pouch.

Captain Agarwal said, "Welcome aboard, Tarendra." He did a double-take. "Hey, you look older now."

"I am," I growled as I saluted him with the bloody dagger.

I didn't kill myself in order to come out here to commit murder, I thought in anger, but as I recognized that thought I was stunned—I had never thought of my last act in System Sol as suicide, and yet that is what I had done. *No, no, that other one back in System Sol committed suicide for my benefit, but I don't bear any of the responsibility.*

How could I hold that idea when I also believed I was the same person? How could they trust me since I was a suicide? Was I really such a deadly meme as they feared?

My wound was forming up into its final shape. It was on my sleeve rather than on my arm, and it took the shape of a heart, young and idealistic, with a dagger stuck through it.

The meaning of it was clear enough to me: I had worn my heart on my sleeve and then suffered the ambush. I had lost something precious related to heartfelt thoughts but gained this mark of passage. My second childhood was already over and my adult accumulations had begun.

I came out of VR and found my monitors had all been enabled: my "Argus eyes" were open within the ship as well as outside. I ignored the impulse to search the ship in order to look outward instead. There below was the little blue world of Galatea. It did not look like much, yet there was still some bit of magic to it after all. Nearby was an orbital transfer vehicle, a draconid-style pion ship cobbled together for travel to and from Prometheus node over near the dim companion star 85B, nearly one light hour away even at close approach. One light second away was *Old Watcher,* the ship containing the hardware that housed Prometheus, or at least the human interface part of Prometheus, and I could see the communication laser beams connecting *Old Watcher* to *Chrysaor.*

As I looked upon all this, my resentment, confusion, and sense of loss faded away. *I did it! I won the race!*

Seven Views of
Galatea

TARENDRA

Tarendra's orbital sightseeing came to an abrupt end when Captain Agarwal called him back to the VR suite.

"New update," said Agarwal, clearly agitated. "We got no end of wonders today. Prometheus has asked that a young colonial be ferried over to him. A particular one — he called for my great grandson by name. Reginald will be tested."

"Tested in the manner that I was tested, sir?"

"Worse than that," he said, "but I hope not. Bitter you be about your test, and I cannot blame you. That gives you a taste of the bitterness that the sky aunties must feel, and theirs often comes agin me, all 'cause my 'test,' such as it was, proved to be laughably easy. The strange fact is we have lost several lives in these tests."

"I see, sir." Tarendra downgraded his own test into more of a hazing.

"Things be so bad now," continued Agarwal, "that all we want is a fast ship home, back to Earth. Most of the sky people have given up. They be waiting in cold-sleep for the time we can be relieved by the ramship wave, still a hundred-sixty years away. I hope I can bargain a draconid starship out of Prometheus, so the returning members can bring

21

back an alien artifact. That might start to make up for things."

"A ship like the Chinese one, sir?"

"Yes, a pion rocket, like the ferry outside. Or even better, a photon rocket — that's what I'm hoping for. We think that with enough stages a photon rocket might break 80-percent of light speed, four times as fast as a ramship. If we can't beg another ship we will have to limp back in the *Chrysaor,* adding more centuries of dislocation for the returnees."

"Will you be among them, sir?"

"I don't know. Sometimes I think I will go, other times I think I'll stay put. And once or twice I've had the notion to take the *Chrysaor* and head further out." He paused for a moment, then shook his head in disgust. "Enough jaw flappin' about the future, right now we must be going."

"Going, sir?"

"Telepresence down on Galatea. We bin't going to waste the fuel or the time to lug us around bodywise."

Tarendra's sensory input abruptly shifted from the VR suite to a surrobot in a closet. In front of him there was another surrobot wearing a robe and a billed cap; this one swept aside the closet curtain and walked out. In walking his surrobot to follow, Tarendra found there was a two second delay.

The room he entered was a log cabin meeting hall dominated by a large rough table with benches. Light came in through a glass-free window. There was a radio desk in the near corner, where sat a man in robes.

"Welcome, sky people!" said the man, rising quickly to tower over them. "How may we—"

"It's me, Agarwal," said the surrobot in front.

"Hello, Captain."

"And this is Tarendra. Just arrived from Earth."

The man's mouth opened and closed as he struggled to form words.

"Is it true?" he gasped.

"Would I lie?"

"Sometimes you joke. Sir."

"Not this time."

"But—*how?*"

"No time."

The tall man recovered his poise and bowed, saying, "We are honored."

"What have I got on?" asked Agarwal.

"The grey robe and ball cap, sir."

"Good enough. Get a tan robe and pith helmet for Tarendra."

"Yes sir," said the man, moving to fetch the items.

Once Tarendra's surrobot had been clothed, Agarwal's said, "Listen, Gil, I'm looking for Reginald, son of Attipat. Seen him around here?"

"No sir, but it is mid-afternoon on Marketday. He might be napping somewhere."

"Damn, I forgot it was Marketday. I go away for a short while and I forget everything. Thanks Gil. Come on, Tar." His surrobot strode out the door and Tarendra set his own hurrying to catch up.

He stepped out onto the alien world. He saw the tan ground stretching out, dotted with log cabins and tents. In one direction a clump of green, marking a woods, and farmlands all around. The size of 85 Peg in the sky was about thirteen percent bigger than Sol in Earth's sky, and Galatea's orbit gave the planet four seasons, each about forty-four local days.

Here was the world previously colonized by the draconids. The light gravity and the thin atmosphere might be exactly like their unknown homeworld, or it might be only the accident of chance. There was a big question about how much terraforming the aliens had performed on the planet. Then there was the erosion of that work: how much atmosphere had been stripped away by the solar wind in the seventy thousand years since the draconids vanished?

Still, the human presence seemed less established than

Tarendra had expected. As they walked along a dirt path winding between cabins, he asked through the surrobot, "Where are we, sir? An outlying station?"

Agarwal's answering voice came through the starship channel. "If you want to ask me a private question, ask me off-line, like this. Okay?"

"Yes sir."

"This is the center of the village, the urban development of the whole planet. The rectenna is behind us, and beyond that is the landing field."

"But everything is so small and primitive," Tarendra said. "I expected to see a town of eight hundred people!"

"Most of us be farmers, scattered out. The village has only about a hundred and sixty people. Of course, that's during the other three days of the week — today is Marketday. Practically the whole planet's here. I hate crowds."

His surrobot was walking again, so Tarendra followed through the village to the market, an open area of dirt with around a dozen booths set up. It looked like a refugee camp to him, with all the people wearing crudely made simple clothes.

Tarendra's perceptions shifted and realigned as he realized the taller figures were younger generations. How strange that parents had children who grew up to be a head taller, and the grandchildren were true light-worlders, a willowy two-heads taller than the Earth-born.

The little ones at hand were stretch versions of Earth children, probably a lot younger than he took them to be. The young people so out-numbered the adults that he was reminded of school outings. Most of the people went barefoot, but the surrobots passed a cobbler at his trade. Activity was slow since they had arrived in that siesta period in the middle of the thirty-eight hour day. Most of the booths had agricultural produce: grains, fruits, vegetables, livestock, milk products. They stopped their surrobots in front of a stall selling alcoholic beverages.

ATTIPAT

A farmer from the furthest outskirts came over to the beer stall. Attipat, the stall's most regular customer, looked up from the bench where he sat.

"Why, hello there," he said. "A long time has passed since I saw you last. Have you heard about it?"

"I have," said the farmer, "but I'd like to hear it from the source."

"Ah," said Attipat. Turning to the barkeep, he said, "There, you see? An appreciative audience."

"He must be the last on the planet," said the barkeep, winking at the farmer.

"To begin at the beginning," said Attipat, "it was a day like today, a Marketday. Different season, yes. And I was here, promoting fellowship, just as I am now.

"Along came the two surrobots. They march right up to me, the one following the other. The first one says it is looking for my son Reginald.

"Now, I had been working at fellowship so hard that day I had become a bit tired and cranky. The proper forms of introduction had not been followed, and I did not know who this was that was talking to me. So to put them in their place, I said, 'Greetings, sky person.'"

"That got him to admit that it was my granddad Owen Agarwal.

"In turn, I admitted a lack of certainty as to the whereabouts of my son. But my mind was busy working, putting two and two together. I was wondering why the sudden interest in Regi, and then it hit me. I said, 'You're gonna take 'im, bin't you? Up into the sky.'"

"He said I was right, and he sounded surprised. He asked me how I knew.

"So I told him, 'Well sir, that's all he's ever wanted, and here you come in your fancy suit, so it stands to reason.' At that point I was inspired to press for a favor of my own, to build on having impressed him, so I asked if he might take me instead.

"He refused, and I'll admit this irked me some, so I asked if he might pay me for the loss of a farmhand when he takes my son. Then I said a few hot words about raising that good-for-nothing boy through twenty-four years of real time.

"Talk of 'real time,' that did it, I tell you. And using Earth years, sure. So the surrobot grabbed me by the shirt here with one hand, and cocked a metal fist with the other. I challenged him to hit me, I did. He let me go and said he would see about paying me. Then he said his coming for Regi was not his choice. I suggested that it was a call from Prometheus, and I did this to egg him into anger, or to impress him with my brilliance. Or both. Or neither. In any event, he said it was a call from a draconid.

"That was the first inkling that something big, something historical, was going on. I thought it was just another day, but it was not. You could have knocked me over with a feather, so I sat down.

"All of a sudden, in my dizziness I wondered who was riding the other surrobot. I asked if it was Bell or one of the aunties, and here came the second shock of the day—

"'No,' says The Captain, 'Bell has been replaced. This is the ship's newest officer, Tarendra. He arrived today. From

Earth.'"

"At that I stood up and saluted the other surrobot. Tarendra spoke then, probably his first words on Galatea. He has a young voice, and he sounded a little embarrassed. He ordered me 'at ease,' and asked for the location of my son. I told him that Regi was with the Horse Eaters. And then they turned and marched off. I tell you, I was stunned at what I had just witnessed, so I turned to our barkeep here and said . . ."

"'Give me another drink,'" said the man. "'I have just seen history—and it passed me by!'"

REGINALD

Agarwal's great grandson Reginald left his homeworld Galatea for the first time. After blasting off in a lander, he transferred to a draconid pion ferry. He rode this for one hundred and fifty hours to meet the aliens, an interview that lasted about forty hours. He rode back for one hundred and fifty hours with a novel proposal: in short, a new interstellar expedition, this one sponsored by the aliens.

The Space Academy, long a dormant dream, came into existence through blood, sweat, and tears. Reginald was at the heart of it for over six thousand hours, when he received a telephone call from Galatea.

"Is this Reginald, son of Attitpat?" asked a female voice.

"Yes. Is that She-Fierce?"

"This is She-Fierce of the Free People."

"Good to hear you! I often think of you. How be you?"

"You have given me a son," she said. "The baby is born."

"The. . . ."

"Hello? Be you there?"

"I am here. I was just surprised. Very surprised."

"Since you left the ground, you lost track of time up

there."

"Well, yes, that is true," said Reginald. "But still, this is sudden."

"Sudden? He was born a few days ago."

"I mean, I am surprised you did not tell me when you first found out you were with child."

"That makes no sense. You would only worry."

"Are you sure he is mine?"

"You will not insult me again."

"Forgive me."

"Only once. Now then, when be you coming back down here?"

"Ah. . . ."

"Hello, be you there?"

"Yes."

"Will you return after a season? After several seasons?"

"No."

"When will you return?"

"I will not return."

"Now I am surprised."

"I am sorry."

"Did you know this plan, that day?"

"I did not know until after I came up here. It was a surprise for me."

"We be both surprised."

CAPTAIN AGARWAL

In the twelfth year of preparation, Owen Agarwal felt trapped in a type of limbo. There were still decades before the expedition would leave. Still sixty-six years before the permission from Earth might arrive.

He thought of his wife Agnes Charan. She had died so long before, at such a young age. In their brief time together she had given him so much good advice. What would she tell him now? Would she allow him to start the expedition without Earth's permission?

He had not married again. This was somewhat surprising to him. He had not thought of himself as a one-woman man, and yet that is how it had worked out.

In the original mission plan, the idea of setting up a colony on Galatea was secondary, only a possibility if the world proved habitable on close examination. It seemed far more likely that they would arrive at 85 Peg, study for a decade, then return to Sol. That was the operational model. Until it was overtaken by events.

There was that moment on the bridge when suddenly everybody knew it. They had not even awakened the Life Survey Team yet. Agarwal was forming a ribald comment, but seeing stiffness and shock in some of those around him, he refrained from such talk. Still, with this new thing in mind he appraised the Rajasthani profile of his First Officer and found much to admire.

But then Chief Sensor Operator Charan reported something, and his gaze turned to her. She glanced up, caught his eyes, and smiled a knowing smile.

And that was it.

He had all sorts of rationalizations after the fact, but they were only rationalizations.

She had chosen him.

Colonization was still only a potential then, a possibility. And now, four generations later, the colony existed, but what would Agnes say if she saw it? Was all their effort worth it? Their descendents would be farmers for the next wave of technological sophisticates. Was her death worth it?

How would she react to the draconids? What would she say to them?

And what would she advise him about the Chinese pion ship speeding toward the colony world that she and he had made? It was forty-five years away. Was it worse to have the coming overlords be Chinese, or was it better?

X.O. SHARAYU PETHWICK

The Galatean man and the Earth woman met in private consultation at the Academy.

"It is difficult to be a person in one's twenties," said sky auntie Pethwick to Reginald. "It is also difficult for a person to manage the distortion caused by hibernation, where one's personal chronology becomes untethered from history. You are suffering both conditions at the same time."

"Yes."

"But you are not the first. I, too, have suffered it. I was in my twenties when we arrived here. I tell you this not to denigrate your suffering, nor to lord it up over you, but to offer you hope and comfort. You are not alone."

"Thank you." He took a deep breath, let it out. "There are many things. At the moment it is about my son. He's, uh, in his twenties now. The age gap between us has narrowed.

"When I talk to him—we have always had a distant relationship, but it seems to be getting worse."

"Go on."

"When he was younger, a child, it was easy for me to talk with him about his life and experience. There was a

33

commonality."

"Yes."

"Even through his teens. But now, now he is nearly at the age I was when I left. When I untethered from history, as you put it. Soon he will be older than I am."

"Surprisingly these feelings are not unknown back on Earth," she said. "A man is a traveling salesman, a trader, and he regrets not being closer to home for the baby's first tooth, the child's first day of school, and such events. You mention the closing of the age gap, and even this is common on Earth, albeit at a slower pace than what you are experiencing."

"How about him being older than me?"

"This is analogous to when the parent steps aside to allow the offspring to lead the family. It is as if you became an elder—"

"Or entered a 'second childhood.'"

"Yes. You say that with bad feelings, but it is true. All part of the human experience."

"You yourself have a limited experience of life on Earth."

"Exactly. Just like your experience on Galatea."

"One difference is that I am being crushed by this simulated gravity you find so natural," said Reginald. "Still, you make a good point. You were twenty, you arrived in this system. What were your thoughts before you left System Sol?"

"Of course I wondered what would happen. I thought, 'Will we spend ten years studying rocks and ice before returning home, or will we discover something more? Microbial life? Fossils?' I was on the Life Survey Team, so I naturally focused on that. I was only an assistant back then."

"Then when they woke you up, it was already much bigger than microbes!"

"In fact a Big Dumb Object, or that is what we thought at the time. My superiors had all sorts of strange terms. It was all purely theoretical, concepts being thrown around in response to this alien thing. First it was a type one, Enigmatic Object. Then it was Monkey Test — no, that was after Rat Maze. Then Ethical Index and Teaching Tool."

"Does Prometheus know you initially called him 'dumb'?"

"Who is going to tell him? You?"

CHIEF ENGINEER RICHARD
KOUNTHAPANYA

Richard Kouthapanya was a light-skinned Dravidian who loved a good fight but was not cruel or brutal. In his twenties he had been the leader of the landing party on the Big Dumb Object. The Chief Engineer back then was Delia Sidhu, an Australoid braggart who always tried to impress everyone with her importance. Making money seemed her obsession, and she always haggled over prices and wages.

Kouthapanya's engineering was more pure than hers, or so he thought.

He studied the image from the latest photon rocket probe. At zero speed, the probe was pointed at the north celestial pole: Polaris marked the center of the forward view. One hundred and twelve stars were visible to the naked eye in a cone of sixty degrees. The star Capella was off to the right; Deneb and Vega to the left.

Engineering was a beautiful art of order, but it was only good for things, not the human heart itself. For example, take the mutiny that nearly tore the early colony on Galatea.

First there were the two couples, then two more women

joined them. At the time, Kouthapanya had laughed to himself since the conspirators could not seem to do the math: the children of each couple could marry the children of the others, but their grandchildren would be marrying cousins if they kept to themselves. Still, the barriers proved to be not as tight as all that: over time some colony people joined the nomads, a few of the nomads settled down into the colony, and the nomad women dallied with colonial men. Something like that had happened with young Reginald a while back, and now he was technically a grandfather.

Kouthapanya looked at another image, this time from the probe under thrust. With sixty-five percent light speed the forward view was largely made up of blue-shifted red giant stars in a clone of clustering.

Out of thirty people, highly screened individuals, it turned out that one was a sadist, while another was both aggressive and accepted violence as a way to solve problems. Then four others were drawn into this orbit of rebellion, making one fifth of the total. To say nothing of Polyphemus, another one of the ancients like Prometheus. Polyphemus became patron of the rebels, but maybe he had planted the idea of mutiny in the first place.

Kouthapanya considered a third image from the probe. Achieving eighty-eight percent of light speed, the forward view was crowded and smaller, thirty-two degrees across, surrounded by black, the beginning of tunnel vision. The blue-shifting has brought new stars into view: the visible one hundred have become over two thousand. Sixty-nine of the earlier ones were now brighter than Vega, and Vega was brighter than Sirius, normally the brightest star. Capella was brighter still, as bright as Jupiter.

Any object can be tested to destruction; any person can be pushed to the breaking point. It might be that the future-rebels had hidden flaws that did not affect their exploration tasks, yet shattered under the strain when colonization came into play. Or perhaps Polyphemus actively bent the will of one-fifth of the people.

Kouthapanya examined a fourth image from the probe. At ninety-six percent of light speed, ninety-eight stars were now brighter than Vega. Many were brighter than Sirius, brighter than Mars. Deneb and Vega were as bright as Jupiter. Capella shone like Venus.

Still, it was mutiny. Kouthapanya was still somewhat surprised Captain Agarwal did not kill the lot of them: his anger had been much quicker in those days, before the experience of parenting had really mellowed him quite a bit. It would have spared a great deal of trouble and bloodshed in those first decades if he had killed them, too, and he probably could have just killed the one and then the others would have stayed in line. But he did not. It would have crippled the colony far worse than their desertion did.

Kouthapanya looked at the last image from the probe. With ninety-nine percent of light speed, the forward cone was now reduced to eighteen degrees: the view from the bottom of a deep well. There was no "starbow": he smiled at remembering that romantic detail of old scientific scenarios predicting multicolored rings of stars, with a darkened central spot. And yet the clustered stars, so close together, shining so brightly, were a new kind of romantic magic.

The mission from System Sol to 85 Peg had been the longest shot of the bunch, an afterthought, really, whose main selling point was having the shortest distance. The three most favored missions were to Ras Alhague, Omega Sagitarii, and Alpha Chameleon, all located within the hydrogen gas cloud of the Frisch Wall, one of the rare structures within the Local Bubble surrounding System Sol. Those stars offered the potential of multiple journeys to neighboring systems, but for the *Chrysaor* it was a tight shot from Sol's Local Fluff to 'the Cinch,' the micro-cloud of hydrogen surrounding 85 Pegasi.

And now they were preparing an expedition to 29 Orionis, the draconid homeworld.

It was 164 light years away. That would be 817 years by ramship, but a photon rocket would cut that down to 193 years, which compared nicely with the original 199-year trip to 85 Peg.

29 Orionis was located beyond the Local Bubble, tucked inside the surrounding wall of Loop 1, meaning it was great territory for hydrogen-scooping ramships. The *Chrysaor* scoop would be depowered and collapsed, put into a streamlining sabot.

A photon rocket was good for one-way voyages. There was a chance that there might be antimatter dumps at 29 Orionis, similar to the ones at 85 Peg.

"Antimatter dumps," what a concept! His Earth self would be boggled, had been boggled. Antimatter medicine and power plants were very stingy with the stuff. Even the pion rocket used a relatively small ratio of antimatter, 1:40, but the photon rocket used a brutal ratio of 1:1. The tons of antimatter being used up to boost a ship to near lightspeed was difficult to comprehend, and it would have been impossible for his Earth self.

Just moving his own body would require eight times his body weight in antimatter.

How many lives could be saved using that antimatter for medicine? How many city-powering plants could be run, for how many centuries?

The scale of it all was stupefying.

ARCHAEOLOGIST YENFEI

As the Chinese pion ship decelerated into System 85 Peg, Doctor Yenfei pondered many things.

How much did the resident Indians know about her ship and its mission? For that matter, how much did the ancient aliens know? It seemed highly probable that the ancient aliens could detect details that the Chinese would rather keep hidden.

But beyond all that cloak and dagger stuff, there was her passion for archaeology. Had the Indians ruined any sites on Galatea? Had the ancient aliens told them where to look? Had all the major sites already been opened?

Seventy thousand years had passed since the marsupial lizardmen had left Galatea. That was an enormous amount of time. For an Earth analogy that meant reaching back to the Middle Paleolithic, in the center of the Fourth Ice Age. Even without the rough treatment of glacier movement, that length of time would presumably erase all traces of a technological civilization. As the old saw said, "Steel lasts for a lifetime, iron for generations, and copper for a civilization, but only flint lasts forever."

And yet Earth had sites showing Neanderthal cave art

from sixty-five thousand years ago. So the lizardmen could have used natural caves or constructed deep repositories to secure important materials. Even the Terracotta Army was purposefully hidden and preserved.

Her mind turned to the children's show "History Wizard," one of her first favorites. In it, the eponymous sage would transit time and cross continents to visit very different peoples and places. Yenfei as a child always had a sense that the wizard was happier when he was anywhere but the contemporary time. Maybe he, too, had a sibling and parents he wanted to escape from. Only later did she realize this was her feeling, and now, across nine decades of time and thirty-eight light years of space, she was liberated from all that.

True, there was still the birthing job, but she was free of competition with her sister and criticism from her mother. They were dust now, and she was History Wizard.

Tarendra
at the
Orion Wall

END ON PLANET 3

It was their last day on the airless post-nova world of Planet 3, the day when the years spent surveying the former draconid homeworld and searching the deep bunkers was either going to succeed or fail. Tarendra stood alone outside the base, watching for the expedition team that was late in returning. The giant sun 29 Orionis had set, and in the twilight of its third planet, the bulbous mushroom-cacti were contracting as the temperature fell from torrid to frozen, and the trilobytes, biomechanical land crabs the size of rats, were swarming as they did every dusk.

Tarendra looked around at the details that had been so wondrous to him before: the crumbling ruins of the squatters, the robotic species who had come long after the place had become a cinder; the cacti and trilobytes, plants and pets the squatters had left behind when they fled a subsequent nebula alert; and the trace remains of the draconids and their garden world from 70,000 years earlier. All of it now spoke to him of failure and wasted effort, with the explorers from Earth and Galatea stranded in the Orion Wall beyond the Local Bubble.

It wasn't supposed to be this way, Tarendra thought.

•

"Mercurian archaeology, what an adventure that will be," Captain Agarwal had said, shaking his head. "And what a motley crew!" He had counted off on his fingers. "A few old timers, Greatest India-persons like you and me; a science section of third century Chinese; a crew of Galatean colonials, including me own great grandson; and a bunch of synthetic draconid revenants. Quite a collection, if I say so myself."

Tarendra had been proud to be considered an "old timer," as if he were a human member of the original crew, rather than an AI who had been born after they had set out.

Tarendra reconsidered the whole thing in terms of simple human analogy. It begins way back when Neanderthals walked the Earth, and a nearby star named Geminga blew out a supernova shell that created the Local Bubble. System Sol found itself near the center of this vast emptiness, hundreds of light years across. The Neanderthals passed away and Homo Sapiens sent explorers from their home oasis of System Sol, walking across the desert to another oasis, 85 Pegasi. Here they discovered Earth-like Galatea, and here they met an ancient entity they called Prometheus. Prometheus gave them a mission and a chariot so advanced that it seemed magical. They rode this photonic vehicle to the distant edge of the Local Bubble desert and found at 29 Orionis the outpost of an interstellar civilization that had existed for millions of years. While the daily technology at System 29 Ori was not much advanced beyond that of the explorers, their cultural wealth was astonishing. So the Solarian explorers were like pastoral nomads who had journeyed to the coast, and upon entering the cosmopolitan city there, they were dazzled by the hardware of skyscrapers and trains, nearly enraptured by the software of institutions and sybaritic luxuries. It was overwhelming. The Solarians were in danger of dissolving like a sugar cube, but not a cube placed in a cup of tea where it would serve to sweeten the whole, rather a cube dropped into a warm pool where it would vanish without a trace.

•

Tarendra's melancholic reverie was broken when the expedition team walked onto the plaza. Their heavy-duty vac suits made them look as robotic as his own surrobot body, but they were biological inside, while his essence was contained within a computer node weighing a kilogram. Even from 50 meters he could tell it was no good. Their radio silence, and their body language spoke volumes. Reginald didn't even kick at the trilobytes.

There was nothing to say. Tarendra went inside the pressure cabin and prepared the galley for food service. After a few minutes they began coming in through the airlock in pairs, starting with Captain Agarwal and XO Sharayu Pethwick.

"Captain," said Tarendra, "the Eosan liason called while you were out."

Agarwal scowled at that. "Leave a message?" he growled.

"They request that you call them as soon as possible."

The Eosans, a civilization of the HabJung, were their biggest creditors, and the explorers did not possess a sufficient amount of their preferred trade soft. So the explorers would probably have to work something out with the other two creditors. But it seemed as though they could never earn enough to buy the 9,200 tons of antimatter for their return trip to System 85 Peg, and time was running out since the next planetary nebula was due to erupt in 90-something years.

The sapient life forms of System 29 Ori were in two groups: the habitat jungle (a ring of orbital habitats surrounding the giant star) and the post-jovians. The HabJung had around two dozen civilizations scattered like embers in the ashes, all together a scant few billion sapients getting on with their lives until the evacuation. The two post-jovians, who initially seemed to be Old One entities like Prometheus, were AI colony minds surrounding stellified gas giant planets. They lived at a greatly reduced speed, which made even simple conversations last months or years. More importantly, the post-jovians had all the antimatter in the system, having made it in a method similar to that used by the Old Ones back in 85 Pegasi: they had it all and were very tight-fisted with it.

As the captain went into the laser booth to call the creditors, the revenants came in through the airlock. Looking at their haunted eyes and gaunt faces, it was hard for Tarendra to remember how cool and sleek they used to be, how their initial aura of self-assuredness and mystery had given them a status of superior "otherness." Their poise had been shattered on Planet 3: the cindered grave of the homeworld that they "remembered" had been occupied by squatters; the draconid legacy, carefully stored in datavaults, had long since been looted by tomb robbers; and there seemed to be no draconids among the billions of soft lifes living in the orbital habitat jungle, nor even any memory of draconids.

In came Reginald, Agarwal's great grandson and Galatean space academy graduate. He did not look so bad to Tarendra, in fact, he looked relieved. The rest of the team came in. Some helped themselves to food and drink: most sat around in the dingy lounge, talking in low voices. The Chinese scientists, who had done such incredible analysis and a fair amount of digging, were sad that this expedition was over. At least they had found an opportunity to shine.

The captain entered the room and Tarendra could tell that something was up.

"I just talked to the Eosans," he said, "and the Hephs and the Wineans. We will sell the last of our entertainment vids to the Eosans to cover part of our debt—the Hephs and the Wineans will cover the rest if we sell them fixed packages of games and music, respectively."

When the Solarian explorers first arrived in System 29 Ori, they were shown all the pomp and circumstance of visiting emissaries. This phase faded away and they found that they were mostly admired for their "barbarian" qualities, and their "barbarian virtues" sent a ripple through the arts. The HabJung studied the explorers' culture and began imitating elements that appealed to them, passing them through the prisms of their own perceptions. At first it was flattering that they seemed to think so highly of the "Sirius Metaculture," as they called it, but the HabJung versions were always strange to the explorers, usually kitschy, but sometimes incomprehensible and other times grotesque parody.

The explorers found that cultural software was all that they had to trade.

"So that should take care of the debt," continued Captain Agarwal. "The problem is that we have very little remaining to trade with those three groups. We have been treating our cultural software like coins, so that our wallet is now mighty nigh empty. We need to create wealth here— we have to work."

"As if we have been playing all this time?" said Dr. Yenfei.

"Yes," said the captain, "we've done work, a heap of great work that just isn't valued. We have proved that this world was bad affected by the nova—we have added to HabJung's data to show that there was a right sharp shock to the system long before 29 Orionis went giant. The megadeath is plain in the archaeological evidence. We have pieced together the epics of the draconid retreat to Planet 4, thence to the belt, and finally to Planet 5. But nobody in this system cares enough to buy the data off'n us."

The local star's expansion into a giant was the hazy dawn of history to the HabJung. The explorers' quest for the draconid legacy was lost in the night before that dawn.

"Since we'll be buying our own antimatter," said the captain, "I shouldn't wonder that we might sacrifice some speed. We came here at eighty-eight percent lightspeed using eight times our ship's mass in antimatter, but we can go back using only two times our ship's mass. That's 2,300 tons of antimatter, and the trip will be just 275 years."

This was a middle way, only 90 years longer than the

fastest way, and much less expensive.

"Now then, how to make wealth." Captain Agarwal started pacing as he continued talking, absently scratching at his salt and pepper beard. "A few of us have wondered if the draconid treasures might have been moved to Planet 5, but this has been a dead end for a couple of reasons— obviously our draconid experts only remember that place in its pre-terraformed state, so they cannot help locate potential sites, and then there is the difficult nature in working on a semi-Venusian world."

For billions of years Planet 5 had been a cold world of Nitrogen atmosphere, but after 11,000 years of its primary star growing giant, Planet 5's orbit became habitable, so with terraforming it would have been a garden world for around 5,000 years before becoming a scalding moist greenhouse.

"We need information on Planet 5. We should comb through all the free data, but we really need to have direct contact with one of the post-jovian entities, or both. I trust the Wineans and I believe them when they say they have begun negotiating with the posties on our behalf for the antimatter, but with the post-jovian frame of time reference being so blasted slow, it is crucial that we get our own people in there directly. Even so, it will probably take ten or fifteen years for them to have a simple chin-chin, but that still gives us a heap of time to head back to System 85 Peg on our original twenty year schedule.

"While our talk team is living in slowtime, the rest of us will be working at making money. The minor stuff will be the 'anthropology circus' we've talked 'bout before. I've got a few leads on cultures in the HabJung who might be interested in folk dance and industrial lore, and that's just for starters. But the big project will be an orbital parasol to put all of Planet 5 in shadow. I've talked with a few outsiders and, as I understand it, the temperature will drop fast, so that the atmosphere will freeze out in 'bout 50 years. We sell the element rights to the highest bidder and that should give us enough for the antimatter—what?"

Chief Engineer Richard Kounthapanya cleared his throat and said,"It is doable to make such a parasol, but I shouldn't wonder the time scale you back-envelope is off by a factor of four."

Captain Agarwal exploded in his typical Bengali anger and demanded that all work it out to his satisfaction right then and there. It took about three hours but he finally accepted that freezing out Planet 5 would take nearly 200 years, and thus would be only completed about a century after the nebula erupted and all the soft lifes, his potential buyers, had fled for System 11 Ori, deeper in the Orion Wall.

He looked so tired to Tarendra at that moment, so haggard.

"Well then, we still have the slow team and the anthropology circus, and we be possibly on the market for some sturdy Venusian landers, if we get any credible leads on where to look on Planet 5."

ROCK BOTTOM

Things were pretty bad then. The Solarians felt it was rock bottom, and while they had a long climb ahead of them, they could each see their part to play and had the belief that things would improve. But it was not really the bottom yet, so when they divided up into their various groups they were actually breaking up the crew.

After they left Planet 3 they encountered feelings of cultural inferiority, as well as the challenge of new diversions which their culture had not prepared them for, and they fell into the "barbarian vices." As children in the candy shop they ran off in different directions, each one alone, and gorged themselves upon different candies. Some of them got sick, a few got very sick. A few got lost and were never seen again. As despair mounted with the years, many chose to hibernate until the word finally came from the Slow Team, the ones sent to meet personally with the post-jovians.

Tarendra no longer kept a Solarian calendar, because it was too depressing, and in dealing with 16 of the 22 HabJung cultures he had to use their systems. He used their languages, too, only using Standard when he would visit the captain at his charity hotel.

Usually Agarwal was sober when Tarendra visited, but almost always he was maudlin. Tarendra would try to talk to him and they would end up arguing about trivia or less. Tarendra was wearing "fleshies" and Agarwal disapproved. There was a horrible sameness to these visits. They were truly at rock bottom, now, and had been there for several years—things would go up a bit, then down again, like the teeth on a saw.

One of Tarendra's visits began in a very typical way. After listening to a litany of complaints, he asked his captain, "What if you made hibernation mandatory?"

"T'would have made things worse," he said. "Just like killing the mutineers on Galatea would have."

"I didn't say 'had made,' I'm not talking about the past, I'm talking about now."

"I heard you," he said, "probably better'n you meant. We still would have lost Reginald, and probably even more than we did."

Always it was Reginald, his great grandson. Tarendra remembered the first time he had met Reginald, then a young man on Galatea in System 85 Peg. They had surprised Reginald in a tent with a young woman, herself a descendant of the mutineers, and the captain gave them a short amount of time to make their goodbyes.

"Did you see that?" he had asked Tarendra, off-line. "She bargained for 18 minutes. We'll give them 12, heh-heh."

"What are they doing, Captain?"

"Oh Tar, be you really so green?" he had said. "They be making babies."

"They *are?*" Tarendra had turned the surrobot's head to look back at the tent. The infrared scan had showed one figure sitting on a camp stool and the other figure. . .a metal hand blocked the view.

"Come on now, Tar, give them some privacy," the captain had said. "At least a few minutes."

Back in System 29 Ori, Tarendra said, "It isn't as though

he were dead."

"You be wrong," said Agarwal. "You mean to say 'He isn't dead,' which is truth, but for us, he is dead."

While only an outpost, System 29 Ori still had a link to the rest of the Perseid Association in the form of a "train station" starbridge: a 3,000 AU-long railgun that launched capsules at .99 lightspeed to be decelerated at another station in System 11 Ori, 76 light years away. Reginald and a few others, including some revenants, had boarded a capsule at the starbridge and blasted out. They had not said anything to anyone else. Apparently they had jumped ship in order to explore further, to travel by interstellar train perhaps as far as the capital system at Lambda Persei, 200 light years distant.

"Maybe he was kidnapped," said Agarwal. "I can believe the revenants would abandon ship like that, but I have a hard time believing that Reginald wouldn't say something. Even suicides leave notes." He paused. "Maybe I should have gone after him. Take one more look over the horizon. Study on it—this system be just an evacuation zone. Imagine what it be like in a regular system of the Perseid Association . . . "

"But our mission requires that we return," said Tarendra.

"Does it?" he shot back. "Why? We sent reports, we beamed a mighty heap of data. So against all that, delivered at lightspeed for nothing, what could we possibly offer by returning?"

"We are not a disposable probe, captain," said Tarendra. "We will return with the first-hand knowledge and experience. As living beings we can answer questions about the data, as well as offer context and interpretation that would be beyond the Sirian—beyond the Solarian conceptual framework. We are witnesses of galactic civilization, more valuable in our selves than all the mindless data we have transmitted."

"Yes," he said. "All right. And so shall ye be going back in all the glory of your fleshie here?"

"Uh, I don't know," said Tarendra, caught off guard. "I haven't thought about it."

"I got to admit that seeing you in these living surrobots is a bit distasteful to me," he said, "but when you wear this—this—"

"Womanform," said Tarendra.

"All right, this *womanform,* I find it disturbing. Distracting."

"I'm just trying it out," said Tarendra. "I have different fleshies for several of the different species here in HabJung—I've swam as a dolphinform in the ammonia oceans of the Cadalioneans, I've scuttled in crabform across the murky floors of methane seas among the Apolloneans." Tarendra was starting to get angry at having to defend his research and himself. "As for my body's gender, you were the one who first thought my name was feminine, so I wonder if you don't have some sort of problem."

"Well, Tar," said Captain Agarwal. "Could you just wear some clothes on this fleshie?"

Tarendra blushed, a searing fire from the top of his face down to a point between his breasts. Suddenly awakened to the fact that he had forgotten his own civilization's nudity-taboo, he thought, *I was* khrgak-ak, *a Hyrieusean making the change from larval form*—no! *I was* slinztlin, *a draconid infant lost in the maternal pouch, confusing down with up*—no!

He had become so engrossed in studying the many aliens that he had become untethered. Even surrobots wear simple clothing, yet he had forgotten that. Was he trying to shock Captain Agarwal out of his melancholy with this fleshie, or was he trying to seduce him? Why did the fleshie, which he had designed with alien hobbyists, look so much like Agnes Charan, the captain's wife, who had died as a colonist back on Galatea of System 85 Peg?

Perhaps Tarendra should have bowed to Agarwal's sensible request and asked to borrow a robe, but his shame was too great for that, so he mumbled apologies and fled. He got rid of his fleshies. He looked up the System 85 Peg calendar and discovered it was Mission Year 585. They had been in System 29 Ori for nearly 60 years.

WORKING PLANET 5

They were late in getting down to Planet 5 and the nebula eruption came early.

It happened while they were working in the peach-colored mud, feeling the hot rain beat down upon their crabform surrobots: the helium-burning star gave a belch that threw off its outer shell. Suddenly the race was on. The balloon of plasma was expanding at around 25 kilometers per second, but still the Solarians had around 470 days before it would reach Planet 5.

That was a very short timetable for archaeological work, however, and they would not have had a chance if it were not for the help received from some of the alien groups who stayed behind even as the great evacuation began. The starbridge continued spitting out capsules bound for System 11 Ori, but the HabJung suddenly sparkled into life as millions of ramships lit up and headed out-system, eating their way through the rich gas of the Orion Wall, aiming for their metacultural core in the adjacent Loop II Wall.

The explorers had three sites to investigate on Planet 5, thanks to the revenants in the Slow Team who managed to squeeze blood from post-jovian turnips. Each site was a natural deep cave formation that had been sealed up. Planet

5's atmospheric pressure was several bars at sea level, and the surface temperature was near 400 degrees C. It was an engineering challenge something like putting a research base at the bottom of an Earth ocean. Then there was the difficulty of cutting through the cave plugs without using brute-force methods like explosives. It was very slow work and they were racing against time.

A funny thing happened when the nebula engulfed Planet 3 at Eruption Day 72. Now that the former draconid homeworld was physically off-limits, their first-hand data was suddenly worth something—in fact, its value was growing like stock in a bull market.

They had the three stations completed on E-Day 457. With only thirteen days remaining before the nebula wave hit, they ferried the revenants down to the planet. Tarendra assumed they would go in, get whatever they could grab, holograph the rest, and then all could leave before the nebula tide hit. But it did not happen that way at all: they went into each deep vault, they came out looking happy but empty handed, then they went back in and lingered for days.

It was an anticlimax for Tarendra. The lingering became torture. If their Chinese archaeologists had been allowed in, they would have wanted to study everything up to the last minute, too, but since they were locked out like the rest, all Solarians were united in their impatience.

The tenth day of this found Tarendra on the surface in a custom surrocrab. From orbit, Captain Agarwal had just finished announcing an ultimatum that the *Chrysaor* would leave on E-Day 469, with or without the revenants. Tarendra was ready to leave, thinking that the place was even worse than Planet 3.

By local terms it was a "clear" day, in that it was not raining, having only a heavy mist below a ceiling of total cloud cover. He was looking out over the distant ocean of scalding water, musing on how the world had once been Earth-like. From the corner of his multifaceted eye he saw the spherical building atop Site 2.

Suddenly there was a loud boom to the side, and the sphere was gone. Tarendra scuttled over to find that it had imploded into a lumpy pancake against the ground. Out in the middle of this wreckage there was a strange swirling of mist in the air, pointing to a pinhole crack into which the atmosphere was pouring. He had to somehow block that flow, so he plugged it with his body.

It seemed to work.

"*Chrysaor,* emergency at Site 2!" he radioed up to the starship.

There was no response. He knew they must be over the horizon.

He was on his own.

"Help!" cried a revenant voice over the radio. "Help! What happened?"

"This is Tarendra. I am at the surface near Site 2. The structure failed."

"This is Manasa," said the voice. "I am down at the bottom of Site 2. I cannot seem to contact the other members. The power is out and I think I am trapped."

With the idea of doing a quick substitution at plugging the hole, Tarendra whistled up a surrocrab from the crabshack. He talked to Manasa as he remotely piloted the machine over to his location, but as it came near, the wreckage shifted beneath him.

Manasa screamed. Tarendra halted the other crab.

"What is the matter?" asked Tarendra.

"The ceiling bent—I thought I was going to die!"

As he made the crab retreat, Tarendra felt he was precariously suspended over a lethal pit. To calm them both down, he said, "This problem reminds me of a time back in India when a girl fell down a well. . ."

Manasa was drawn into the story of how the unfortunate child was freed by men digging an escape shaft, and the two sketched out a plan to rescue her that involved an airlock and a new tunnel.

"Agarwal to Tarendra, what's happened at Site 2?"

Tarendra explained the situation.

"Tar, I want you to get off that spot. We can't risk you."

"If I move, Manasa will be killed, and I might also die."

"Hang in there, Tar. We will move to a geo-stationary orbit."

Tarendra set the surrobots to tunneling and tried to work out the "airlock" part. It would be on the surface, at the top of the tunnel.

Once the ship achieved a new orbit, Agarwal and others used telepresence to pilot crabs. The tunnel was forming rapidly, but the airlock was proving to be difficult.

Chief Engineer Kounthapanya said, "Look, we can't make one."

"What if we have the lock at the bottom?" asked Tarendra.

"That does not help us. Unless, hmm. . . "

"What?"

"Unless we have the lock climb down there and climb back."

"That sounds impossible," said Tarendra.

"Unless we rig a crab to carry a person inside."

"I see! But wait, we still have a problem getting the person into the crab-lock without being crushed by the pressure."

"So we bury the crab-lock before it breaks through at the bottom," said Kounthapanya.

"Great!" said Tarendra. "Then what?"

"It digs into the habitat, the person enters, and then it digs its way up."

"And somewhere in there, the wreckage finally gives way, plunging me into the abyss."

"We will have a scaffolding bridge to hold you up."

They had the plans, but their telepresence skills were weak, so Tarendra did most of the detail work while they did simple things.

When the crab-lock was ready, Tarendra remotely drove it down the tunnel. Rather than burying the thing, they had affixed a metal skirt that would act as a docking ring. Tarendra told Manasa to get set, and when he received her ready signal, he broke through the habitat wall.

The pressure pulled the crab-lock in, but the skirt held, stopping the flow. Manasa crawled into the cramped confines of the jury-rigged escape vehicle.

The moment had arrived. Everyone was tense.

Tarendra disengaged from the skirt and started clawing up to the surface, against the stream of atmosphere pouring down. The skirt dilated closed, stopping the stream, but up on the surface the wreckage shifted beneath Tarendra, making his anchor line go taut. He focused on piloting the crab-lock up. Meter by meter he climbed, worried for the safety of Manasa. He felt that saving her would be somehow saving the girl in India, his first love, whom he could no longer remember with any detail.

Then Tarendra was falling and he lost consciousness.

When he came up out of reset, he found himself halfway down a pit. Above him a chain of surrocrabs were hauling him up.

"Wait—what?" he said. "What about Manasa? Is she all right?"

"She's fine, she's fine," said Captain Agarwal. "We took over and brought her up the last stretch. You did all the hard work."

At last they pulled Tarendra up onto solid ground.

"Damn, Tar, that was close!" said Agarwal. "Blame our hobbyists for faulty design. But hey, I've got to give credit to you—those crabforms made it all possible, the construction and the rescue. Good job!"

A few simple words, but it felt like validation to Tarendra, like he was an "old timer" again.

•

The evacuation of the other stations was quickly completed. After the lander brought the last members aboard, they lit up the *Chrysaor*'s fusion rocket. They were behind schedule so the expanding nebula was gaining on them for several hours (they watched it engulf Planet 5 from a distance), but after 14 hours of acceleration they had matched velocity, and then began to pull ahead.

They went to the closer post-jovian to withdraw their antimatter account. The posties had accelerated to realtime in order to study the nebula, so the explorers did not have a time lag with them anymore. True to form, the captain started bargaining with the posties. Some of the alien friends who were accompanying the *Chrysaor* like a small flotilla wanted permission to visit System 85 Peg, but they were concerned about going slow enough to avoid arriving there before the Solarians did. So Agarwal bargained with them, too, and through it all found his way up to a full 9,200 tons of antimatter. Before long they were headed back to 85 Pegasi at a cruising velocity of .88 lightspeed.

RETURN TO SYSTEM 85 PEG

About ten years into the return flight the Solarians received a report from System 85 Peg, relayed from Earth, telling of radio contact with a group of "Far Neighbors." This group was in Sagittarius of the Loop III wall, 305 light years from Earth in the direction of the galactic core, at a right angle to the direction of Orion where the explorers were coming from. Earth had received this message in M.Y. 430, which was nearly a century before the *Chrysaor* had arrived at System 29 Ori. So Earth already knew something about civilizations outside of the Local Bubble a few centuries before the explorers sent their first report.

The return voyage was nearly half complete when they got a message from System 85 Peg telling the Solarians that their mother civilization had finally faded away. New civilizations had risen up on Sol's worlds and in Sol's orbital habitats, but none of them were technocentric as theirs had been. System Sol was turning inward.

The explorers wondered what they would find at System 85 Peg. It seemed likely to be a remnant that would either quickly die or fossilize.

In M.Y. 786 they entered the system, having been away for 453 years. Things seemed lively from what they could see.

Prometheus debriefed the explorers in VR near his asteroid. Captain Agarwal was older, 65 or 70 biological. Tarendra was older, too, and his VR persona looked rather like Dr. Ramanathan, his old mentor back in India, but X.O. Pethwick said he looked a bit like Agarwal.

After all the official reports were given, there was a period of informal conversation.

"Friend Owen," said Prometheus, "you have met success, it seems."

"If you say so," said Captain Agarwal.

"Your voice betrays some doubt inside your heart," said Prometheus.

"Well, sure," said Agarwal. "The civilization that sent us out no longer exists. Our reports have 'bout as much impact at System Sol as fantasy tales, I reckon, yet we sweated and struggled, even died for it."

"I cannot speak for System Sol, alas," said Prometheus. "Yet here your work has made profound effect. You introduced the Local Bubble to galactic cultures, them to us as well."

"But you Old Ones could have just told us everything," said Agarwal. "In a certain light, the trip to 29 Orionis looks like a wild goose chase."

"With great respect I disagree, old friend," said Prometheus. "The things we could have told you, might have told you, were older than your species—obsolete. As well, these things would all be tainted by our own perceptions, dark suspicions held. Should we have filled you with our loss and sent you out to Sagittarius to hunt the authors of Geminga, Star of Death? The answer must be no, I have to say. The supernova can be made by Fate or by design, as must be clear by now to you who have seen the stars made from gas giant planets. The same technique can make a weapon star."

In surprise, Tarendra asked, "The Geminga supernova—the formation of the Local Bubble—was a deliberate act?"

"Perhaps," said Prometheus, "but far more deadly are the memes that spread like ripples at the speed of light to bring the hearing ones to early death."

Pethwick asked, "Was our civilization destroyed by memes off'n the Sagittarian Far Neighbors?"

"I do not think this was the case for them," said Prometheus. "You must remember that no culture lasts forever, even when it seems it must. At last it falls and others rise to grow." Prometheus paused, then continued. "You mourn the past now—it is fitting, apt. But let me speak to you about a birth, a culture strong and vibrant, shared among the eight colonial worlds but centered here. Though Earth is gone, her daughter now can crawl.

"For centuries we built a way to live based largely on the common values shared between AI and human beings both. This culture we term *homonoia* now.

"We owe you scouts a debt profound and true. Should any of you wish to now retire, you will receive a princely sum for life. We hope that some will stay, advising us on all the challenges we face today. To celebrate your safe return to us, as well as honor your accomplishments, do we propose a formal name for all—the 'Homonoia of Solaria,' and call this year the first of Unity."

"Leaving the Mission Year dating system?"

"That is correct," said Prometheus. "A new beginning date for our new culture born among the stars."

While Prometheus was talking Tarendra had the dawning sensation of being able to see a forest with all the trees: *We found at 85 Pegasi the remains of a once-interstellar civilization, and while we had gradually assumed the mantle, we had also sought to locate the originals, the draconids. Searching for knowledge of their fate but also legitimacy for a Solarian role in the Local Bubble, claims of territory by any others, either the draconids or their successors.*

There were no claims—for the Perseid Association in the Loop II wall of Orion, the Local Bubble was seen as an undesirable wasteland, just like all the Loop interiors where gas clouds for ramships to feed upon are few and far between. There were no heirs to the draconids— or, rather, we Solarians were the rightful and uncontested heirs. We hope to avoid the inward turning of the Earth AIs, we hope to avoid the AI overlordship we saw in 29 Orionis, but we will strive to achieve with our Close Neighbors the same sort of interspecies harmony we had witnessed in HabJung.

All in all they had a heroes' welcome. The tasks ahead were daunting, but Tarendra was eager to begin working on them. It really was great to be back home.

ABOUT THE AUTHOR

Michael Andre-Driussi is mainly known as a Gene Wolfe scholar, beginning with *Lexicon Urthus* (1994), but he has also published a number of stories collected in the post-apocalyptic *Fallout Stories* (2016), the Martian mashup of *The Jizmatic Trilogy* + (2017), the devilish *Old Flames Burn Manvi* (2017), and the touristy *Doomsday and Other Tours* (2018).

www.ingramcontent.com/pod-product-compliance
Lightning Source LLC
Chambersburg PA
CBHW020551130626
46552CB00007B/2856